Freddy the Very Adventurous Ferry

by **Rozy Abra**

Illustrated by André Ellis

Published by Not Very Limited

Freddy is a ferry.

He likes his home in Falmouth.   He has lots of friends.   But...

Freddy is not happy.

Each day he takes people from Falmouth to Flushing.
Then he takes them back again.

All day, he goes   backwards and forwards.
                        backwards and forwards,
                                                 across the harbour.

It is hard work.

Freddy wants to travel over Oceans
                                    and sail across Seas .

Freddy wants to see the World.

One day, Freddy saw a big white ship in the harbour.

She was being repaired.

Freddy watched as he went

backwards and forwards,
backwards and forwards,

across the harbour.

Some men mended her engines.
They mended the dents in her hull.
They painted her hull with fresh white paint.
They fitted new seats on her deck.
They polished her brass until it shone.

Everybody worked hard until the big white ship was ready to go to sea.

One day,   when Freddy woke up,   she had...

...gone.

Freddy saw Tommy Tug   towing a trawler   into the harbour.

"Tommy",   called Freddy.   "Where is the big white ship?"

"She sailed for Penzance this morning",   Tommy replied.
"She is called the Scillonian.
She's a Very Important Ferry."

"She's a ferry like me?"   Freddy asked, feeling very surprised.

"No, not like you Freddy",
    said Tommy,

    and he hooted
    with laughter
    in a very rude way.

    "She's a proper ferry.
    She's a sea-going ferry.

    She sails every day
            from Penzance
                    to the Scilly Isles,   across the open sea.
    You couldn't do that.   You're far too small to go to sea."

Freddy slipped away, feeling very sad.
    He felt ashamed.   "Too small to go to sea",
    he said to himself.

"What kind of ferry can I be,   if I am too small to go to sea?"

Early next morning,
Freddy slipped away from his mooring.
He headed out of the harbour   to the open sea.
Freddy was gone
before any other boats were awake.

Freddy had never felt so happy before.

The sun was warm on his cabin.   The waves washed against his sides
and splashed across his decks.

A seagull   dived
        down
        through
        the air
    and settled on the sea   beside him.

"Freddy",   she called.
"Freddy,   you're too far from Falmouth   to be safe.
        Go home!
        Go home, before it's too late".   Then she flew away.

Freddy felt offended.

     "I don't see why   I should go home",   he said to himself.

     "I know what   I'm doing.
     I know where I'm going.

     I am a sea-going ferry now.
     I am off   to the   Scilly Isles!"

Soon Freddy saw the islands on the horizon.

Some friendly seals watched Freddy arrive.

"Hello, Freddy Ferry.
We have seen you in Falmouth",   shouted the seals.
"Why are you so far from home?"

But Freddy did not reply.

He liked the Scilly Isles.
He liked the clear blue sea.
He liked the white sandy beaches.
He wanted to stay.

It was very peaceful.

Freddy felt   s l e e p y.   Gentle waves rocked him   from side   to side.
Freddy fell a s l e e p . . . . .

A seal
woke him up
when the tide
turned.

She began to bark at Freddy,
her eyes wide with worry.

"Wake up, Freddy.
The tide has turned.
Soon the sun will set.
The weather changes quickly here.
Go home now, before it's too late."

Freddy decided it was time to go.

He wanted to tell his friends
he was a big ferry now.
He had crossed the open sea.

Freddy pulled up his anchor.

He started his engine.
He began to head for home.

Then Freddy heard a cry

"*HELP !!*   We can't swim!"

Two children were floating   out to sea on an airbed.
The airbed was drifting towards some rocks.
Freddy knew that when it hit the rocks it would   *BURST !!*

The children would drown.

"I'll save you!" he shouted. "Freddy to the rescue!"

Freddy revved up his engine ...

Soon he was s p e e d i n g
across the waves
to save them.

When he reached the children, they climbed
on board.

Freddy took them to the shore. The children thanked him
and ran home.

Freddy felt very pleased with himself.

"Lucky I was here to rescue them",
he said. "I am as good as a lifeboat now!"

The sun had set.   It was nearly   dark.

Freddy set off   for home.

He was beginning   to feel   afraid.

How would he
            find his way
                        home
                        in the dark?

The sky was black.

He could see no stars.

The wind was beginning to blow.
The waves were getting bigger.

Freddy's engine   was working

very **hard** **pushing** him through the heavy seas.

Soon the wind blew away the clouds.   Stars sparkled in the black sky.
The moon came out.   A silver beam shone   across the sea.

Freddy could see the way to Falmouth.   He began to feel brave again.

But ... a few minutes later ... his engine stopped ...   The only sounds ...

16

were the wild wind and the heavy seas ... Freddy stopped feeling brave.

Then far away,
Freddy heard the

chug chug chug of a very big engine.

Tommy Tug   had come to tow Freddy home.

Now it was Freddy's turn   to be rescued.

"Thank you   for saving me" whispered Freddy.

He was feeling small and very silly.

As Tommy towed him
      towards the quay,

Freddy saw all the boats waiting for him.
Freddy wished he could run away.

He was sure to be in trouble for going to sea.

He was sure the other boats would hoot with laughter
                  because he needed to be towed home.

But all the other boats began to cheer! A big flag across the quay said

about Freddy saving the children. "Well done, Freddy, you were very

"WELCOME HOME, FREDDY THE HERO"! The Harbourmaster had heard

brave", he said. "But please don't go away again. We need you here!"

Back at Freddy's mooring,   Rosie Rowing Boat   was waiting.

"Oh Freddy"   said Rosie.   "Don't you know   we all need you
to carry everyone   between Flushing and Falmouth?
You are a silly ferry."

"No" said Freddy. "I'm not a Scilly ferry.
I'm the Flushing ferry.

It's been fun   having an adventure,
but in future   I shall stay   at home."